CENTURY ORIENTAL 世纪东方

练习与测试 初级

朗文 视听说 英语教程

· Angela Blackwell · Jay Maurer · Irene E. Schoenberg ·

TRUE COLORS

中国电力出版社
www.centuryoriental.com.cn

京权图字：01-2003-1574

图书在版编目(CIP)数据

TRUE COLORS 朗文视听说英语教程(初级) 练习与测试/(美)布莱克威尔(Blackwell,A.)著.
北京：中国电力出版社，2003
ISBN 978-7-5083-1574-4
Ⅰ.T… Ⅱ.布… Ⅲ.英语，美国－听说教学－习题 Ⅳ.H319.9-44
中国版本图书馆 CIP 数据核字(2003)第 062763 号

Authorized translation from the English language edition, *True Colors 1_Workbook and Achievement Tests*, by Angela Blackwell, published by Addison Wesley Longman, Inc. 10 Bank Street, White Plains, NY. 10606.

ENGLISH/SIMPLIFIED CHINESE language edition jointly published by PEARSON EDUCATION NORTH ASIA LTD. and CHINA ELECTRIC POWER PRESS

This edition is authorized for sale only in People's Republic of China (excluding the Special Administrative Regions of Hong Kong and Macau)

True Colors
朗文视听说英语教程(初级)
练习与测试

著：(美) Angela Blackwell

责任编辑：王春红
出版发行：中国电力出版社
社 址：北京市西城区三里河路 6 号(100044)
网 址：http://www.centuryoriental.com.cn
印 刷：北京密云红光印刷厂
开本尺寸：215mm × 275mm
印 张：6.5
字 数：104 千字
版 次：2003 年 8 月第 1 版 2007 年 5 月第 4 次印刷
书 号：ISBN 978-7-5083-1574-4
定 价：9.80 元
版权所有 翻印必究
如有印装质量问题，出版社负责调换。联系电话：010－62193493

Contents

Are you in this class?

1 Complete the conversations.

Fill in the blanks with words from the box. You can use some words more than once.

I'm	He's	She's	We're	They're	It's

1. **A:** This is Bob. _____He's_____ my neighbor.

   B: Hi, Bob.

2. **A:** Where's Susan?

   B: _____ in the car.

3. **A:** Hi! _____ Alison.

   B: Nice to meet you, Alison.

4. **A:** I'm Kate, and this is Emma. _____ in this class.

   B: Hi. I'm Tom.

5. **A:** How old is Mike?

   B: _____ nine.

6. **A:** Where's the English class?

   B: _____ in room 208.

7. **A:** Who's that?

   B: Adela. _____ Ron's wife.

8. **A:** What do you do?

   B: _____ an engineer.

9. **A:** Where are your friends?

   B: _____ in New York.

② Write sentences.

Look at the pictures. Write a sentence for each picture. Use words from the box.

| a doctor | a secretary | an engineer | a nurse | a lawyer | a homemaker |

1. ____He's an engineer.____

2. _____

3. _____

4. _____

5. _____

6. _____

③ Unscramble the conversation.

Put the conversation in the correct order.

_____	So what do you do, Sally?
___1___	Sally, this is my friend Steve.
_____	I'm an engineer.
_____	Hi, Sally. Nice to meet you.
_____	I'm a teacher. What about you?
_____	Nice to meet you, too.

❹ Write about yourself.

Answer the questions. Tell about yourself. Use short answers.

Example: Are you tall? <u>Yes, I am.</u>

1. Are you short? _____

2. Are you a teenager? _____

3. Are you a student? _____

4. Are you single? _____

5. Are you from the United States? _____

6. Are you married? _____

7. Are you athletic? _____

8. Are you studious? _____

❺ Complete the sentences.

*Fill in the blanks with **a**, **an**, or **the**.*

1. Sandra is _____<u>a</u>_____ doctor.

2. _____<u>The</u>_____ doctor's name is Felix Yamamoto.

3. Carlos is _____ student at San Fernando College.

4. _____ students in my class are all very nice.

5. He's a nurse? But he's _____ man!

6. _____ new teacher is very young.

7. My friend is _____ artist. He's very good.

8. That's a beautiful picture. _____ artist is Paul Cummings.

9. I live in _____ United States.

6 Match descriptions and pictures.

Look at the pictures. Match each sentence to the correct picture. Write the correct letter in the blank.

a. They're good friends.   **b.** They're married.   **c.** She's studious.

1. _____   2. _____   3. _____

Challenge

7 Read and answer questions.

Read the postcard.
Then write the correct answer in the blank.

1. The postcard is to _____ Danny _____.
   Jeff / Mexico / Danny

2. The postcard is from _____.
   Danny / Danny's teacher / Danny's mother

3. Danny lives in

   _____.
   Los Angeles / Berkeley / Mexico

4. Danny is

   _____.
   a student / a lawyer / a doctor

Beach

Ruins

Hi there!
   Mexico is beautiful!
Our hotel is really nice. The
people are friendly, and the
old Mayan ruins are
fascinating. And we love the
beaches! See you on the 17th.
Good luck with your classes!
   Love,
   Mom

March 10, 20--

Danny Leaver
1313 Washington Street, # B
Berkeley, CA 94703

8 Write addresses.

Write the addresses on the envelopes. Pay attention to capital letters.

Note: Illinois = IL   California = CA   Ohio = OH

1. john henry / 2034 rutherford road / champaign il 61821 / usa

2. andrea martin / 140 mission drive / arcadia ca 91006

3. alan mansell / personnel department / worldnet, inc. / 2000 arlington street / columbus oh 43220

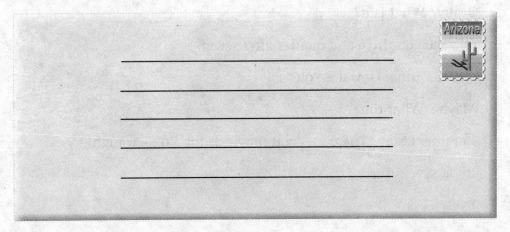

There's a noise downstairs!

❶ Circle the correct time.

Look at the clocks. Circle the correct choice.

1. **a.** It's four o'clock.
   b. It's a quarter to four.

2. **a.** It's three-fifteen.
   b. It's three forty-five.

3. **a.** It's two forty-five.
   b. It's a quarter to two.

4. **a.** It's noon.
   b. It's twelve-thirty.

❷ Unscramble the conversation.

Put the conversation in the correct order.

__1__	Hello?
_____	*Fatal Love.* Do you want to go?
_____	Great! Bye!
_____	Hi, Monica. This is Anna.
_____	Really? What is it?
_____	OK. See you there at a quarter after seven.
_____	Oh, hi, Anna! How are you?
_____	Maybe. What time?
_____	I'm fine. Listen. There's a good movie at the Roxie tonight.
_____	It's at seven-thirty.
_____	Bye!

❸ Write answers.

Look at the calendar pages.

WEDNESDAY JULY 7
6 pm meeting at school

THURSDAY JULY 8
8 pm movie Roxie Theater

FRIDAY JULY 9
7:30 play Palace Theater

SATURDAY JULY 10
2:30 rock concert at the park

SUNDAY JULY 11
3:00 baseball game on TV

Answer the questions.

1. Where is the meeting? _It's at school._

2. What time is the meeting? _It's at 6:00._

3. What time is the movie? _____

4. Where is the movie? _____

5. What time is the rock concert? _____

6. Where is the play? _____

7. What time is the baseball game? _____

8. What time is the play? _____

9. Where is the rock concert? _____

❹ Complete the sentences.

*Fill in the blanks with is or **are**.*

1. There _____is_____ a good movie on TV tonight.

2. There _____are_____ three girls in my family.

3. There _____ twenty computers in the school.

4. There _____ a burglar in the house.

5. There _____ water on the table.

6. There _____ a good play at the theater.

7. There _____ three bedrooms in the house.

8. There _____ milk in the glass.

9. There _____ rice for dinner tonight.

⑤ Match questions and answers.

Match the questions with the answers.

1. __d__	What movie is at the Lido tonight?	**a.** I'm fine.
2. _____	I'm Allen. What's your name?	**b.** It's ten to seven.
3. _____	Are you married?	**c.** It's at the Palace Theater.
4. _____	Is he married?	**d.** *Fatal Love.*
5. _____	What time is it?	**e.** I'm Paul, and this is Cindy.
6. _____	Where's the concert?	**f.** Yes, I am.
7. _____	How are you?	**g.** No, he isn't. He's single.

⑥ Rewrite a message.

Write the message with correct punctuation.

hi julie
how are you theres a great movie at the roxie its called *true love* its at six oclock do you
want to go with me
sara

⓻ Read and answer questions.

A. *Look at the advertisement for a movie. Answer the questions. Use short answers.*

Questions	Answers
1. What movie is it?	Loving You.
2. What time is the movie?	
3. Who's in the movie?	
4. Where is the movie?	

B. *Now write your own questions about this movie.*

Questions	Answers
1. _____?	*Escape from Philadelphia.*
2. _____?	Kurt Costner.
3. _____?	At the Galaxy Theater.
4. _____?	At 1:10, 4:30, and 7:50.

8 Write sentences.

A. *Circle the things that you see in the picture.*

supermarkets   (water)   trees   restaurants

a theater   a museum   a zoo   an airport

a university   schools   houses

Challenge

B. *Now write sentences about the picture. Use **there is** and **there are**.*

Example:	There is a museum in the picture.

1. _____

2. _____

3. _____

4. _____

5. _____

For computer questions, press one now.

❶ Identify the speaker.

*Who is speaking? Write **teacher**, **mother**, or **friend**.*

 teacher

 mother

 friend

"Open your books to page 47."

1. _____ teacher _____

"Don't be late for dinner."

2. _____

"Please help me with my homework."

3. _____

"Do page 24 for homework."

4. _____

"Be home at 11:00 P.M.!"

5. _____

"Don't tell my mother!"

6. _____

❷ Match beginnings and endings.

Find the second part of each sentence. Write the correct letter in the blank.

1. ___b___   We're not at home. Please leave   **a.** late.

2. _____   Jeannie, call   **b.** a message.

3. _____   Do you want to go   **c.** a video tonight.

4. _____   Do you have a problem? Talk   **d.** for a walk?

5. _____   Let's watch   **e.** to the teacher.

6. _____   Don't hang   **f.** your mother.

7. _____   Don't be   **g.** up! Stay on the line.

❸ Complete the conversation.

*Fill in the blanks in the conversation. Use **Let's** or **Do you want to**.*

A: ___Do you want to___ go out tonight?
              1.

B: Good idea. How about a movie?

A: OK. _____ go to the Roxie.
              2.

B: What's playing at the Roxie?

A: I don't know. _____ look in the newspaper. . . *Fatal Love.*
                      3.

_____ see that?
      4.

B: No, not really. Forget the movie. How about a restaurant? _____ eat out?
                                                                        5.

A: Sure. Where?

B: How about Enrico's? It's Italian. It's good.

A: OK. _____ walk?
              6.

B: No, I'm tired. _____ drive instead.
                      7.

❹ Complete the sentences.

Fill in each blank with a possessive adjective.

1. Ellen is in _____her_____ room.

2. I can't go out now! _____ hair is wet!

3. This is for Tom. _____ birthday is tomorrow.

4. Give me that! That's _____ book!

5. Hello. I'm Patty. What's _____ name?

6. My parents are out tonight. It's _____ wedding anniversary.

7. Today is _____ birthday. I'm six.

8. Hi. I'm Manny, and this is _____ wife, Sylvia.

9. The children are at the movies with _____ friends.

10. What a pretty cat! What's _____ name?

❺ Rewrite sentences.

Rewrite the sentences with the correct punctuation.

1. its johns birthday on monday

   _____It's John's birthday on Monday._____

2. marys party is on wednesday

   _____

3. thats mr johnsons house

   _____

4. its my parents anniversary tomorrow

   _____

5. the childrens party is next friday

   _____

❻ Write sentences.

Look at the pictures. Write sentences with possessive nouns.

David

Samantha

Alex

mug

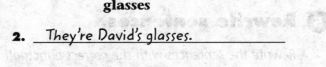

glasses

1. ___It's Alex's mug.___

2. ___They're David's glasses.___

armchair

CD player

3. _____

4. _____

T-shirt

newspaper

5. _____

6. _____

⑦ Complete the puzzle.

Look at the pictures. Write the correct word or words across each line. What's the extra word?

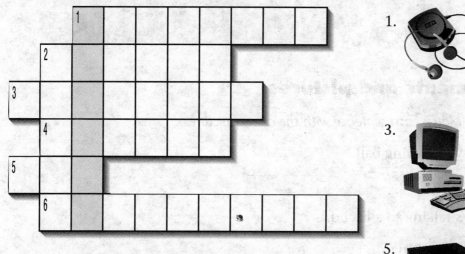

1.

2.

3.

4.

5.   6.

The extra word is _____.

⑧ Write the answers.

Look at the family tree. Then answer the questions.

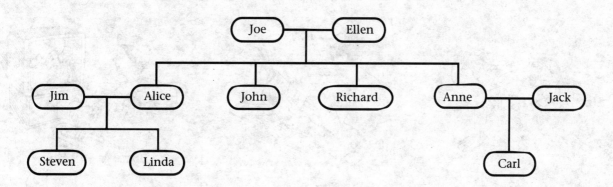

1. Who is Joe's wife? _____ Ellen _____

2. Who are Richard's sisters? __Alice__ and __Anne__

3. Who are Ellen's daughters? _____ and _____

4. Who is Linda's grandfather? _____

5. Who are Alice's brothers? _____ and _____

6. Who is Carl's grandmother? _____

7. Who is Alice's son? _____

What's Bob doing?

❶ Match statements and pictures.

Look at the pictures. Match each sentence with the correct picture.

1. ___e___   They're playing ball.

2. _____   He's studying.

3. _____   She's talking to a friend.

4. _____   He's exercising.

5. _____   He's fixing the car.

6. _____   She's watching TV.

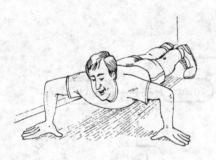

a.

b.

c.

d.

e.

f.

② Complete the sentences.

Complete each sentence with the correct word from the box. Use some words more than once.

playing	doing	going	making	watching

1. I'm _____doing_____ my homework.

2. We're _____ tennis.

3. I'm _____ dinner.

4. He's _____ for a walk.

5. They're _____ a video.

6. They're _____ baseball.

7. Amy is _____ TV.

8. Mom is _____ pizza.

③ Complete the paragraph.

Look at the picture. Write the correct form of the verb in the blank.

It's Saturday afternoon in Bellville. The sun _____is shining_____. The Munson

                                                1. shine

family is at home. Gloria Munson _____ a book. Her son Peter

                                                2. read

and his friend _____ basketball. Alice, her daughter, _____ on

                3. play   **4. talk**

the phone. Baby Anne _____. Gloria's husband, Tom, _____ a

                          5. sleep   **6. fix**

bicycle. Adam, from Sal's Pizza, _____ a pizza. Two people _____

                            7. deliver   **8. walk**

down the street. The Munson's neighbors _____ their car.

                                          9. wash

4 Write questions.

Alice is talking to her grandmother in Florida.
Read their conversation. Write the questions.

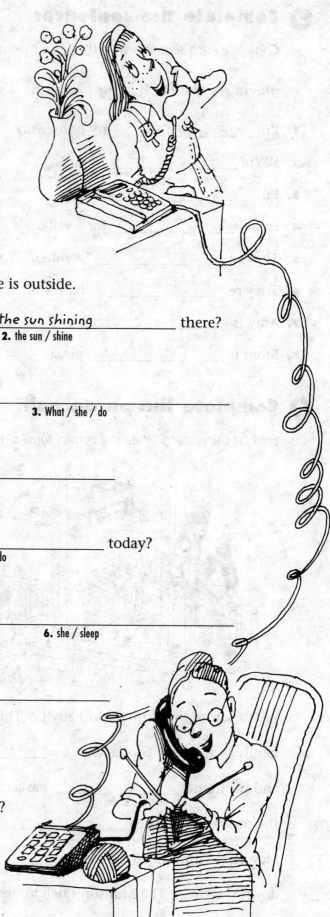

A: Grandma? This is Alice.

B: Alice! What a nice surprise! Hello, dear.

_____What are you doing?_____
1. What / you / do

A: Oh, nothing.

B: Where are you?

A: I'm at home. I'm inside. But everyone else is outside.

B: Outside? It's raining here. _____Is the sun shining_____ there?
2. the sun / shine

A: Yes, it's a beautiful day.

B: And what about your Mom? _____
3. What / she / do

A: She's reading.

B: That's nice. _____
4. What / she / read

A: A new book.

B: And your Dad? _____ today?
5. What / he / do

A: He's here. He's fixing his bike.

B: That's good. How's the baby? _____
6. she / sleep

A: Yes, she's sleeping now. She's fine.

B: And Peter? _____
7. What / he / do

A: He's with his friend Mario.

B: _____
8. What / they / do

A: Playing basketball. What about you, Gran?

_____
9. What / you / do

B: I'm making a sweater for your baby sister.

5 Write ordinal numbers.

Unscramble the words.

DRITH   _____third_____   TOURFH   _____

THENT   _____   NOSCED   _____

THIFF   _____   THISX   _____

THINN   _____   STIRF   _____

VENSETH   _____   THIGHE   _____

6 Complete the sentences.

Write the correct object pronouns in the blanks.

1. Where's Anne? There's a phone call for _____her_____.

2. John, listen to me! I'm talking to _____!

3. That's my book! Give it to _____!

4. My homework? I'm doing _____ now.

5. Alice and John? We're meeting _____ tonight.

6. My sister's in Kenya. I'm writing a letter to _____ now.

7. We're watching a movie. Come and watch it with _____!

8. That's a good book. We're reading _____ in class.

9. The children are going to the baseball game. Let's go with _____.

10. Anita is at Luigi's Pizza, and Josh is with _____.

11. You're going to New York? Is your wife going with _____?

12. We're lost. Please give _____ directions.

7 **Write answers.**

A. *Look at the map.*
Then answer the questions that follow.

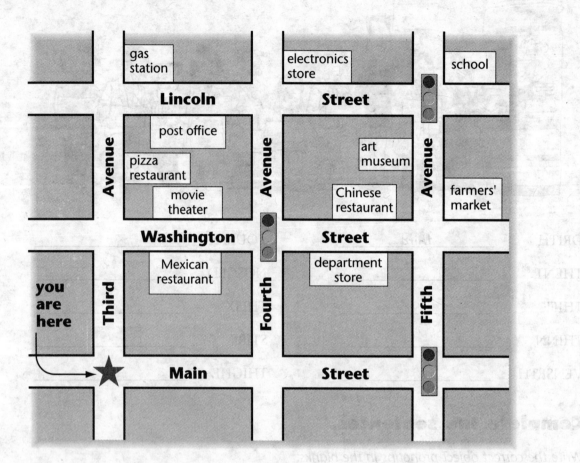

1. Where is the electronics store?

It's on Lincoln Street, at the corner of Fourth Avenue.

2. Where is the gas station?

3. Where is the Mexican restaurant?

4. Where is the Chinese restaurant?

5. Where is the farmers' market?

B. *Now read the directions. Start at **Main Street and Third Avenue.***

1. Walk down Main Street to Fifth Avenue. Turn left. It's between Washington Street

and Lincoln Street, on the left.

What is it? _____It's the art museum._____

2. Go down Third Avenue to Lincoln Street. Turn right. It's between Third Avenue and

Fourth Avenue, on the right.

What is it? _____

3. Go to the corner of Main Street and Fourth Avenue. Turn left on Fourth Avenue.

Go one block. Turn right on Washington Street. It's between Fourth Avenue and

Fifth Avenue, on the right.

What is it? _____

4. Walk down Main Street to Fifth Avenue. Turn left on Fifth Avenue. Walk two blocks.

It's on the right, on the corner of Lincoln Street and Fifth Avenue.

What is it? _____

5. Go down Third Avenue to Washington Street. It's on Third Avenue, between

Washington Street and Lincoln Street, on the right.

What is it? _____

You lose it. We find it.

❶ Choose the correct verb.

Complete the paragraph. Circle the correct form of the verbs.

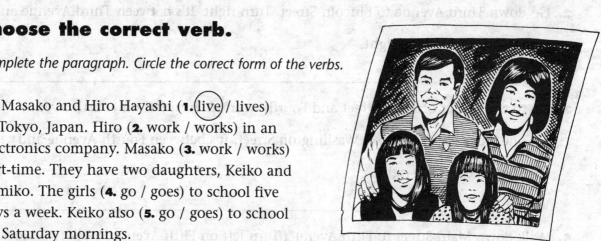

Masako and Hiro Hayashi (**1.** live / lives) in Tokyo, Japan. Hiro (**2.** work / works) in an electronics company. Masako (**3.** work / works) part-time. They have two daughters, Keiko and Tomiko. The girls (**4.** go / goes) to school five days a week. Keiko also (**5.** go / goes) to school on Saturday mornings.

The Hayashis (**6.** eat / eats) breakfast at 6:30. Hiro (**7.** take / takes) the train to work at 7: 30. The girls (**8.** leave / leaves) for school at 8:00. Then Masako (**9.** do / does) the shopping. Sometimes she (**10.** visit / visits) a neighbor. Then she (**11.** make / makes) dinner for the family. In the evenings, the girls (**12.** do / does) homework and (**13.** watch / watches) TV. Hiro often (**14.** come / comes) home late.

❷ Match questions and answers.

A. Match the questions with the answers.

1.	__d__	What's your name?	**a.** No, part-time. I work full-time.
2.	_____	Do you study full-time?	**b.** Not really. It's a hard job.
3.	_____	What do you do?	**c.** In Belmont. It's near San Francisco.
4.	_____	Do you like your job?	**d.** Alex.
5.	_____	When do you work?	**e.** I'm a taxi driver.
6.	_____	Where do you live?	**f.** Yes, I have a son.
7.	_____	Do you have children?	**g.** Five days a week, twelve hours a day.

B. *Now put the words in the correct order to make six questions about Alex. Then answer the questions, using the information on page 22. Use short answers.*

<table>
<tr><td align="center">**Questions**</td><td align="center">**Answers**</td></tr>
</table>

1. Alex / do / does / What

What does Alex do ?   _He's a taxi driver._

2. Alex / Does / full-time / work

_____   _____

3. he / does / Where / live

_____   _____

4. work / When / he / does

_____   _____

5. have / he / a / Does / daughter

_____   _____

6. his / he / job / Does / like

_____   _____

❸ Check the boxes.

A. *What do you think about these subjects? Put checks (✔) in the boxes.*

	Easy	**Hard**	**Interesting**	**Exciting**	**Boring**
art					
business					
computers					
dance					
journalism					
math					
medicine					
music					

(continued on next page)

B. Now write five sentences.

I think art is exciting.

1. _____

2. _____

3. _____

4. _____

5. _____

❹ Write questions.

Read the sentences. Then write questions to complete the conversation.

1. **A:** _____Where do you work, Anna_____?

   B: I work in the library at City University.

2. **A:** _____ your job?

   B: Oh, yes. I love it.

3. **A:** _____ full-time?

   B: No, part-time.

4. **A:** _____?

   B: I work from ten to two.

5. **A:** _____?

   B: I live on 35th Street. It's only five blocks from the university.

❺ Write verbs.

Write the third person singular form of each verb in the simple present tense.

1. look ___looks___   2. drink _____   3. teach _____   4. study _____

5. love _____   6. get _____   7. have _____   8. do _____

9. live _____   10. watch _____   11. worry _____   12. speak _____

6 Write about Carmen and Anna.

A. Look at the pictures. Fill in the charts.

Carmen's house

Anna's house

	Carmen	Anna		Carmen	Anna
1. has a child	✔		**5.** loves to cook		
2. studies part-time			**6.** plays tennis		
3. has a dog			**7.** plays guitar		
4. loves to travel			**8.** wears glasses		

B. Now write about Carmen and Anna.

Carmen

Carmen has a child.

_____

_____

_____

Anna

Anna studies part-time.

_____

_____

_____

7 Write about yourself.

A. *Answer the questions. Tell about yourself.*

Example: Do you study full-time? ___No, I study part-time.___

1. Where do you live? _____

2. Do you live in an apartment? _____

3. Do you live alone? _____

4. What do you do every morning? _____

5. What do you eat for breakfast? _____

6. When do you eat lunch? _____

7. What do you do in the evenings? _____

8. Do you exercise? _____

9. Do you watch TV? _____

10. Do you like music? _____

B. *A pen pal is a person who lives far away. Pen pals write letters to each other.*
Write a postcard to a new pen pal. Write about yourself. Use some of the information
from above. Sign the letter with your name.

Dear pen pal,

   My name is _____ and I live in _____

_____

I_____

_____

_____

_____

_____

                    Sincerely,

                    _____
                    (Sign your name here.)

Review

1 Complete the questions.

*Fill in the blanks with **Do**, **Does**, **Are**, or **Is**.*

1. _____Do_____ you like your job?

2. _____Is_____ there a concert tonight?

3. _____ it raining?

4. _____ you have a computer?

5. _____ Alex have children?

6. _____ there a post office on Washington Street?

7. _____ you married?

8. _____ they working today?

9. _____ Mario like school?

10. _____ you have grandchildren?

11. _____ there a farmers' market here?

12. _____ Peter work full-time?

2 Match verbs and objects.

Draw lines from each verb to one or two words in the circle.

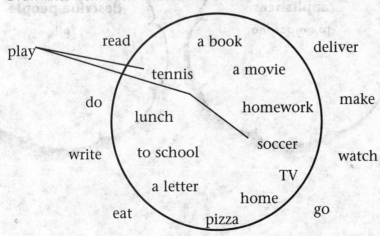

play

read · a book · deliver

tennis · a movie

do · homework · make

lunch

write · to school · soccer · watch

a letter · TV

eat · home · go

pizza

❸ Complete the conversation.

Fill in the blanks with the correct words from the box. Use each word only once.

at	~~from~~	of	on	to

A: John? Is that you? Listen. We're lost.

B: Well, where are you calling ___*from*___?
1.

A: We're _____ the corner _____ Fifth and Main Street.
2. 3.

B: OK. Go _____ the light. Turn left. We're the third house _____ the right.
4. 5.

A: OK. Thanks. See you soon!

Challenge

❹ Test your memory.

Take five minutes. Write more words in each category. How many do you remember?

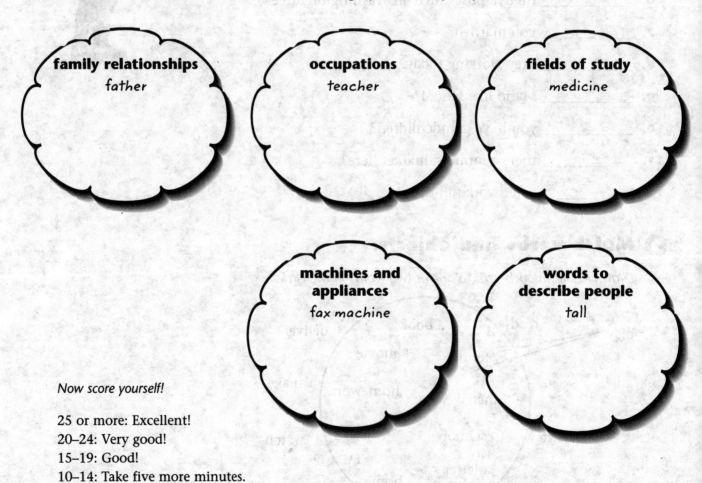

family relationships
father

occupations
teacher

fields of study
medicine

machines and appliances
fax machine

words to describe people
tall

Now score yourself!

25 or more: Excellent!
20–24: Very good!
15–19: Good!
10–14: Take five more minutes.
1–9: Look at Units 1–5 again.

5 Write the expression.

Write the correct expression for each picture.

Let's go to a movie.   ~~Sorry I'm late.~~
Nice to meet you.   We're lost.

1. _Sorry I'm late._

2. _____

3. _____

4. _____

6 Rewrite sentences.

Rewrite the sentences with the correct punctuation.

1. theres a movie at the roxie on wednesday

There's a movie at the Roxie on Wednesday.

2. he doesnt work on saturdays

_____

3. mrs clark is peters grandmother

_____

4. anna is at marias house

_____

We're going to win.

❶ Write vocabulary words.

Label the parts of the body.
Use the words in the box.

back	**ankle**	**elbow**
arm	**hand**	**shoulder**
knee	**wrist**	

1. _____

2. _____

3. _____

4. _____

5. _____

6. _____

7. _____

8. _____

 Question: What other parts of the body can you name?

_____

❷ Complete the sentences.

*Complete each sentence. Use **be going to** and the indicated verb. Use contractions with the pronouns.*

1. He ____'s going to buy____ a book.
$\qquad$ (buy)

2. She _____ a letter.
$\qquad$ (write)

3. She _____ a phone call
$\qquad$ (make)

4. They _____ a movie.
$\qquad$ (watch)

5. They _____ soccer.
$\qquad$ (play)

6. It _____ .
$\qquad$ (rain)

❸ Write questions and answers.

Look at Barbara's calendar for tomorrow.

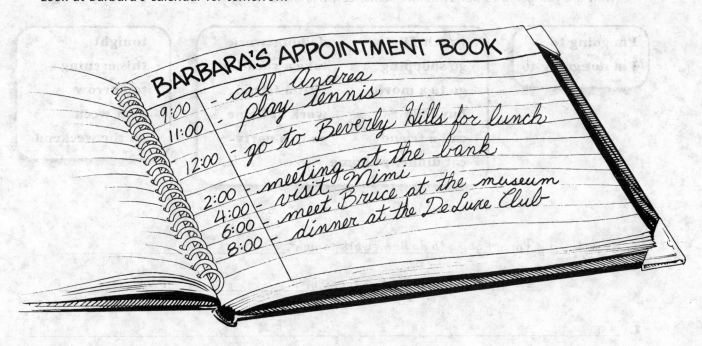

BARBARA'S APPOINTMENT BOOK

9:00 - call Andrea
11:00 - play tennis
12:00 - go to Beverly Hills for lunch
2:00 - meeting at the bank
4:00 - visit Mimi
6:00 - meet Bruce at the museum
8:00 - dinner at the De Luxe Club

Make questions from these words. Then answer the questions.

Questions	Answers

1. What / do / nine o'clock?

   What's she going to do at nine o'clock?   She's going to call Andrea.

2. What / do / eleven o'clock?

   _____   _____

3. Where / go/ twelve o'clock?

   _____   _____

4. Where / be / two o'clock?

   _____   _____

5. What / do / four o'clock?

   _____   _____

6. Who / meet / six o'clock?

   _____   _____

7. Where / go / eight o'clock?

   _____   _____

4 Write about yourself.

What are you going to do? Write five sentences. Use these words:

I'm going to	watch TV	do homework	tonight
I'm not going to	go shopping	take a vacation	this evening
	go to a movie	visit a friend	tomorrow
	buy food	work at home	next week
	call a friend	go to a party	on the weekend
	eat dinner at home		

Example:
I'm not going to do homework tonight.

I'm going to watch TV this evening.

1. _____

2. _____

3. _____

4. _____

5. _____

5 Unscramble the conversation.

Put the conversation in the correct order.

___1___ Doctor's office. Can I help you?

_____ Bye.

_____ Hello, my name is Sarah Lee. I need to see Doctor Martin.

_____ How about four o'clock tomorrow afternoon?

_____ You're welcome. See you then. Good-bye.

_____ Yes. How about eleven o'clock?

_____ Tomorrow afternoon? I'm going to be in class until five. Is the morning a possibility?

_____ Eleven o'clock is fine. Thank you.

6 Complete the sentences.

*Fill in the blanks with **in** or **at**.*

1. Call me. I'm _____ at _____ home now.

2. My mother is _____ work.

3. Angela lives _____ the city.

4. Sarah's not _____ school today. I think she's sick.

5. My husband is _____ home today. He's looking after the children.

6. I'm _____ class until 12:00, but I'm free after that.

7 Rewrite sentences.

Rewrite each sentence, using the adverb in parentheses. Be careful with word order!

1. I have coffee in the morning. (always)

   I always have coffee in the morning.

2. My husband exercises in the morning. (often)

   _____

3. He stays home until 2:00 P.M. (usually)

   _____

4. He goes shopping. (sometimes)

   _____

5. I am at home before six o'clock. (usually)

   _____

6. We watch a movie on TV. (occasionally)

   _____

7. We are in bed before eleven. (never)

   _____

8 Write about yourself.

Use the words from the box. Try to use at least three different words.

always	often	usually	rarely	sometimes	never	occasionally

Example: (have headaches)   I *sometimes have headaches.*

1. (go to bed before eleven o'clock) _____

2. (take a bus to work or school) _____

3. (sleep late on Saturdays) _____

4. (have toothaches) _____

9 Read and answer questions.

A. Read the article from the **Cascadia Times** and fill in the chart on the next page.

Cascadia Times

New Year, New Starts

What are you going to do differently next year? Here are some people's answers:

Liana Hoffman (27)
Ithaca, New York
I'm going to get more exercise. I'm going to walk to work every day. It's only eight blocks from my home, but I always take the bus. Not next year! I'm also going to take an exercise class after work, with my friend Sue.

Amy Williams (15)
Terre Haute, Indiana
I'm going to help my mom more. She's a working mom, and she's often tired. I'm going to clean my room and take the dog out every day…and wash the dishes in the evenings!

Tony Soto (31)
Chico, California
I spend too much time on my computer. I have lots of friends on the Internet but no friends in my life! So I'm going to try a dating service…and make some new friends.

What is she/he going to do?		
Liana	Amy	Tony
1. get more exercise	1.	1.
2.	2.	2.
3.	3.	
	4.	

B. *Read the article again. Write* **T** *(true) or* **F** *(false).*

1. __F__   Liana is a student.

2. _____   Now, Liana takes the bus every day.

3. _____   Now, Amy helps her mom a lot.

4. _____   Amy often washes the dishes now.

5. _____   Tony has a girlfriend.

Can you dance?

❶ Write about yourself.

*Write sentences with **I have to** or **I don't have to**.*

Examples: get up early ___I have to get up early.___

go to work ___I don't have to go to work.___

1. study for exams _____

2. buy food for my family _____

3. speak English in class _____

4. wear a uniform every day _____

5. do homework _____

6. work on the weekend _____

uniform

❷ Write sentences.

Mike is having a party tonight. But nobody can come!
*Write sentences with **have**, **has**, **have to**, or **has to**.*

1. Tom / headache ___Tom has a headache.___

2. Melissa / study for a test ___Melissa has to study for a test.___

3. Amy / work late tonight _____

4. Trisha / sore throat _____

5. Carl and Pete / do homework _____

6. Thomas and Alicia / date _____

7. Leroy / fever _____

8. Keiko / help her mother _____

3 Write answers.

A. Tell about yourself. Use short answers.

Can you cross your eyes?

Example: Can you drive? ___No, I can't.___

1. Can you sing well? _____

2. Can you cook? _____

3. Can you cross your eyes? _____

B. Now write some sentences about yourself.

Example: ___I can't dance well.___

1. _____

2. _____

3. _____

Challenge

4 Read and answer questions.

Read the text and answer the questions about the United States.

In the United States, all children have to go to school from age six to age sixteen. Some schools, especially private schools, have uniforms, but most public schools do not. When they finish high school, American teenagers get a high school diploma. If they want to go to college they have to take the SAT exam.

In the United States you can vote and get married at age eighteen and drive a car at age fifteen or sixteen. You have to take a test before you can get a driver's license.

1. At what age do children have to go to school? ___Six.___

2. Do all students have to wear uniforms at school? ___No.___

3. Do all students have to take an examination when they finish high school? _____

4. At what age can you get married? _____

5. At what age can you drive a car? _____

⑤ Read and match.

A. *Who wrote the invitations? Write a letter below each invitation.*

a.   b.   c.   d.

To: Becky

Come to my birthday party!

When: Saturday August 14, 3 P.M.

Where: 1164 Moncada Drive

RSVP

Dear Mary,
There's a dance at the
Senior Club on Wednesday.
I need a partner, and I
know you like to waltz.
Can you come with me?
Regards,

1. __c__   **2.** _____

Memo

Tony:
How about a game of
tennis tonight? We can
meet at my office at
6:00 P.M.

Hi Jody—
Let's go to Rock City
tonight! There's a new
band playing, and it's
free!

3. _____   **4.** _____

B. *Read the replies. Write the number of the correct invitation under each reply.*

JIM:
I CAN'T MEET AT 6 P.M.
BUT WHAT ABOUT LATER?
6:30? I'D LOVE A GAME.

Hi CARY,
SORRY BUT I CAN'T.
I HAVE TO STAY
HOME TONIGHT TO
HELP MY MOM.
WHAT A BUMMER.

a. invitation number: _____3_____

b. invitation number: _____

Dear Edward,
Thank you so much
for inviting me!
I can't dance
very well, but I'd
love to go to the
dance with you.

Dear Susie,
I can come
to your
party.
Love,

c. invitation number: _____

d. invitation number: _____

6 Unscramble the conversation.

Put the conversation in the correct order.

_____ I am. This chemistry homework is really hard. Can you help me?

_____ Well, can you help me later?

_____ Sure.

___1___ What's the matter? You look worried.

_____ Yes, but not now. I have to wash my hair.

_____ Thanks a million.

Read the article.

Whiz in a Wheelchair

He can't walk, but he can move pretty fast in his wheelchair, and he's training to go even faster. Fifteen-year-old James Parker is a table tennis champion, and he likes wheelchair racing, too!

James was in a bad car accident at the age of six. Now he cannot use his legs, and he has to use a wheelchair. James "drives" the chair with his arms. He also plays video games, and in the summer he plays basketball with his brothers.

But his favorite place is at the table tennis (Ping-Pong) table. James practices every day for an hour after school. "I want to win a gold medal," he says. "I'm sure I can do it. And I want other kids like me to think that they can win, too."

James's house has a special ramp so that he can go in and out of the house easily. At Adams High School in Champaign, Illinois, James is a popular student. He works hard, although he has to sit at the back of the classroom because of his chair. He doesn't mind that at all. "I like it back there," he says. "The teachers can't see me."

a champion

a Ping-Pong table

a wheelchair   **a car accident**

a medal

a ramp

Now write a list of things that James can do.

1. He can move pretty fast in his wheelchair.

2. _____

3. _____

4. _____

5. _____

Do you want some pizza, Lulu?

1 Unscramble the conversation.

Put the conversation in the correct order.

_____	Forty dollars.
_____	Yes? How can I help you?
_____	Do you have any jackets?
___1___	Excuse me.
_____	This red one is nice. How much is it?
_____	Forty dollars? I'll take it.
_____	Sure. Follow me.

2 Complete the sentences.

*Fill in the blanks with **some** or **any**.*

1. I need _____some_____ shoes.

2. I don't have _____any_____ money.

3. I want _____ ice cream.

4. There isn't _____ pizza left.

5. There are _____ good restaurants on Clay Street.

6. There's _____ water on the table.

7. Michael doesn't have _____ brothers or sisters.

8. Please give me _____ information.

9. There aren't _____ good movies at this theater.

10. We don't have _____ homework tonight.

11. She wants _____ coffee.

12. Sorry, I don't have _____ money.

❸ Find the words.

Todd is talking to his friend.
Read what he says. Then draw arrows
to the words one and ones refer to.

"It's my birthday tomorrow. I'm going

to be ten. And I'm going to get some presents!

I hope my grandma gives me some running

shoes. The **ones** I have are too small. And

I want black **ones**.

"And I'm getting a science computer game like the **one** that Mario has. It's a really

good **one**. But you have to go to a special store. The **one** in Glenwood is pretty good.

It's a special **one** just for computer games."

❹ Complete the conversations.

Fill in the blanks.

1. **A:** I need _____an_____ umbrella. Do you have umbrellas?

   B: Sure. Right this way.

   A: I like this black _____one_____. How much is _____?

   B: Twelve dollars.

   A: OK, I'll take _____.

2. **A:** I need _____ socks. Do you sell socks?

   B: Sure. Right this way.

   A: I like these blue _____. How much are _____?

   B: Seven dollars.

   A: OK, I'll take _____.

5 Write vocabulary words.

Label the clothes in the picture. Use the words in the box.

pants	1. _shirt_
sweater	2. _____
~~**shirt**~~	3. _____
glove	4. _____
socks	5. _____
boots	6. _____
skirt	7. _____
belt	8. _____
blouse	9. _____
panty hose	10. _____
shoes	11. _____
raincoat	12. _____

6 Circle the word.

Circle the word that does not belong.

1. nightgown   pajamas   (gloves)
2. skirt   (baseball cap)   dress
3. socks   mittens   gloves
4. shoes   shorts   socks
5. dress   raincoat   umbrella
6. briefs   undershirt   belt
7. bra   suit   panties
8. sport shirt   mittens   dress shirt
9. nightgown   boots   sandals
10. underwear   boxer shorts   coat

7 Write about yourself.

Answer the questions. Use short answers.

Example: Do you have a pair of sandals? <u>Yes, I do.</u>

1. What size shoes do you wear? _____

2. Do you often wear running shoes? _____

3. Are you wearing a sweater right now? _____

4. Do you have an umbrella? _____

5. Do you have a baseball cap? _____

6. Do you have to wear a tie to work? _____

7. Are you wearing a belt right now? _____

8. Do you wear gloves in the winter? _____

Challenge

8 Rewrite sentences.

A. *Rewrite each sentence, making the underlined words and phrases* **plural.**

1. I have <u>a problem</u>. <u>I have some problems.</u>

2. Is that your <u>CD</u>? <u>Are those your CDs?</u>

3. He wants <u>a tie</u> for his birthday. _____

4. There's <u>an umbrella</u> over there. _____

5. There isn't <u>a doctor</u> here. _____

6. Do you have that <u>book</u>? _____

B. *Now rewrite these sentences, making the underlined words and phrases* **singular.**

1. I love those <u>sweaters</u>. <u>I love that sweater.</u>

2. Those <u>T-shirts</u> are the large ones. <u>That T-shirt is the large one.</u>

3. Those <u>books</u> are very good. _____

4. She wants some <u>CDs</u>. _____

5. These <u>movies</u> aren't interesting. _____

6. <u>They</u> are good ones. _____

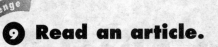

9 Read an article.

Read the article. Then write the correct name under each pictue.

Teens Talk about Style

With so many different "looks" to choose from nowadays, today's teens can choose the look they like best. And it doesn't have to cost money. We asked four teenagers to give us their views on fashion.

Rebecca (16)

I think it's important to be comfortable. I shop at thrift stores, where you can find lots of really cheap clothes. Then I mix and match. I wear big shirts with skirts, or old jeans with a pretty blouse. I like to be comfortable. It's stupid to pay $100 for a pair of jeans.

Don (14)

I wear shorts all year because they're comfortable. I live in San Diego, so it doesn't get very cold. My parents are OK about it. Kids in school think it's normal. I almost never wear a suit.

Jess (15)

I like to wear casual clothes: pants and sports shirts, usually. I have a blue jacket. I wear it everywhere. My brother wears really big pants. I hate that. I think it looks stupid. Girls don't like it either.

April (17)

I like black. Everything I have is black. I wear black pants and sweaters, or a black dress and boots. I even have black pajamas that my mom gave me for Christmas. They're so cool! I have a lot of different jewelry, too.

1. ___Don___ 2. _____ 3. _____ 4. _____

Weren't you at Alice's?

❶ Rewrite sentences.

Rewrite each sentence in the past tense.

1. It's a beautiful day.   <u>It was a beautiful day.</u>

2. That's my boss.   _____

3. We're not at home.   _____

4. There's a party on Saturday.   _____

5. She's not at work.   _____

6. That sweater isn't very nice.   _____

7. There are twelve students in my class.   _____

8. You're late.   _____

9. He's a good swimmer.   _____

❷ Write about yourself.

Answer the questions. Use short answers.

Example: Were you in class yesterday?   <u>Yes, I was. or No, I wasn't.</u>

1. Were you at home the day before yesterday?   _____

2. Was it cold in your city yesterday?   _____

3. Were you at a party last weekend?   _____

4. Were you hungry this morning?   _____

5. Was there an English test last week?   _____

❸ Complete the conversation.

Complete the conversation between a boy and his mother.
Use words from the box. Use the words more than once.

was	wasn't	were	weren't

A: Look at this photo, Mom! Is that you?

B: Sure it is.

A: Where was that?

B: That _____was_____ in Africa.
1.

A: Africa? When _____were_____ you in Africa?
2.

B: In 1974 and 1975.

A: _____ Dad there, too?
3.

B: No, he _____.
4.

A: Wow! _____ it hot there?
5.

B: Yes, it _____. Hot and wet. But it _____ great.
6. 7.

A: Who are those people in the picture?

B: Well, let me see. That guy. . .his name _____ David. He _____
8. 9.

my boss at the time. We _____ both in the same town.
10.

A: And who are those people?

B: They _____ our neighbors. We _____ friends with them.
11. 12.

A: And this guy? Who's that?

B: His name _____ Paul. He _____ my boyfriend.
13. 14.

A: Your boyfriend? But where _____ Dad?
15.

B: Dad and I _____ married then.
16.

❹ Complete the sentences.

Fill in the blanks. Use words from the box.

assistant	boss
fiancé(e)	neighbors
partner	roommate

1. The person you are going to marry is your ___fiancé(e)___.

2. The people who live near you are your _____.

3. The person in charge at work is your _____.

4. The person who helps you at work is your _____.

5. The person who lives in an apartment with you is your _____.

6. The person who owns your business with you is your _____.

Challenge

❺ Unscramble the conversation.

Put the conversation in the correct order.

_____ At home. Why?

___1___ Jenny, where were you last night?

_____ Jason.

_____ There was a party at Anita's house.

_____ Yes. He was gorgeous!

_____ Kate and Jordan...and some of Anita's friends from work...and there was a really nice guy from the university.

_____ I know. He was my boyfriend last year!

_____ Oh, yeah? What was his name?

_____ Really? Who was there?

_____ Jason? Was he tall, with blond hair?

6 Complete the conversations.

*Write the questions. Use **was** and **were**.*

1. A: (Where / you last night?)   _Where were you last night?_

    B: I was at a movie.

2. A: (Who / in it?) _____

    B: Michelle Pfeiffer and Brad Pitt.

3. A: Sounds good. (it / a love story?) _____

    B: No, actually, it was a comedy.

4. A: (Who / with you?) _____

    B: Just some friends. Oh, yes! There was a woman from Boston there. She knows you.

5. A: Really? (What / her name?) _____

    B: Judy.

6. A: Judy? (tall, with glasses?) _____

    B: Wow! She was my roommate in college.

7 Choose the correct word.

Circle the correct word.

1. Those shoes are (my / (mine)).

2. John, where's ((your) / yours) book?

3. (My / Mine) mother works at the supermarket.

4. Give that sweater to Charlie. It's (his / hers).

5. Is that (your / yours) house? It's very big!

6. No, this one is (our / ours).

7. Children, come on in! (Your / Yours) dinner is ready.

8. Jeff and Rick are (our / ours) neighbors.

9. Whose shoes are these? Are they (your / yours), Kate?

10. That bike is (my / mine).

11. Our computer isn't the same as (their / theirs).

8 Read and find differences.

Look at the picture. Then read the text. Find five differences between the text and the picture. Circle them.

I remember my grandmother's living room well. There was a big sofa, and there were (two) comfortable chairs. It was quite dark, because there was only one window. And there were a lot of plants. There was an old piano in one corner of the room. A photo of my grandfather as a young man was on the piano. My grandfather was so handsome! There were other photos on the wall, and I think there was a big picture of the ocean. There was a bookcase full of books, and a clock on the bookcase. But the clock was broken: It was always five o'clock!

My plane just landed.

❶ Write the verbs.

A. *Write the simple past tense form of these verbs.*

1. do ___did___
2. come _____
3. take _____
4. feel _____
5. play _____

6. go _____
7. say _____
8. call _____
9. meet _____
10. make _____

11. tell _____
12. get _____
13. find _____
14. see _____
15. hear _____

B. *Now fill in the blanks. Use the simple past tense forms above. Use each verb only once.*

1. I ___took___ the bus to work this morning.

2. Evan _____ the police when he saw the accident.

3. We _____ to Hawaii on vacation last year.

4. I _____ my homework at five o'clock.

5. I _____ my wife for the first time when we were in college.

6. "Come over here!" she _____.

7. We _____ basketball for two hours last night.

8. I _____ that movie last week.

9. My grandparents _____ to this country from Japan.

10. My brother _____ this sweater in Ireland.

11. I lost my watch, but I _____ it today.

12. When my grandfather died, I _____ very sad.

13. We stayed home last night, and my mom _____ pizza.

14. I _____ Beth about the party, but she didn't go.

15. We _____ beautiful music coming from my son's room.

2 Write words and sentences.

A. Fill in the blanks. Use the words from the box.

| CDs | cars | computers | phone | plane | movies | supermarkets | TV |

It's the end of the 20th century, and our lives are fast. People drive _____cars_____.
1.

We travel around the world by _____. We use _____ at work, and
2.   3.

we shop in _____. We don't write letters very much. Instead, we talk on the
4.

_____. For entertainment, we don't play music or tell stories: We go to
5.

_____, watch _____, and listen to _____.
6.   7.   8.

B. Now write negative sentences.

Three hundred years ago, life was different. In 1700,

1. cars _____*People didn't drive cars.*_____

2. plane _____*People didn't travel around the world by plane.*_____

3. computers _____

4. supermarkets _____

5. phone _____

6. movies _____

7. TV _____

8. CDs _____

❸ Write questions and answers.

*Write **did** or **were**. Then answer the questions. Tell about yourself.*

Example: ___Did___ you get up early this morning? ___No, I didn't.___

___Were___ you at home last night? ___Yes, I was.___

1. _____ you at school today? _____

2. _____ you watch TV last night? _____

3. _____ you on vacation last month? _____

4. _____ you have coffee this morning? _____

5. _____ you go to the supermarket yesterday? _____

❹ Match beginnings and endings.

Look at the calendar. Then finish the sentences.

May

Sunday	Monday	Tuesday	Wednesday	Thursday	Friday	Saturday
				1	2	3
4	5	6	7	8	9	10
11	12	13	(14)	15	16	17
18	19	20	21	22		
25						

Today is Wednesday, May 14th.

1. ___f___   May 13th was   **a.** last month.

2. _____   May 8th was   **b.** last week.

3. _____   May 12th was   **c.** a few days ago.

4. _____   April was   **d.** the day before yesterday.

5. _____   May 4th–10th was   **e.** last Thursday.

6. _____   May 11th was   **f.** yesterday.

⑤ Unscramble the conversation.

A. *Put the conversation in the correct order.*

_____ Sounds like fun. I love tennis. How was the food?

_____ What did you do?

_____ Yesterday morning.

___1___ Hi, Jim! When did you get back?

_____ We played tennis, and we went swimming every day.

_____ So how was Hawaii?

_____ Terrific!

_____ We did! We're going to go back again next year.

_____ Delicious! We had fresh fish every day.

_____ Sounds like you had a great time.

B. *Now write the questions for these answers.*

1. A: ___Hi! When did you get back?___

B: Last night.

2. A: _____ New York?

B: It was great. We had a wonderful time.

3. A: _____?

B: Oh, the usual tourist things . . . we saw the

World Trade Center, and we went to Broadway, and we saw a play. . . .

4. A: _____?

B: Delicious, of course. But the restaurants were pretty expensive.

5. A: _____ weather?

B: Cold and rainy! But we had a good time anyway.

6 Read and answer questions.

A. Read about Brad Pitt. As you read, look for the answers to these questions.

1. Where was he born? _____

2. Did he graduate from college? _____

3. What movie began his career? _____

4. How much money does he make for one movie now? _____

5. Does he like to give interviews? _____

William Bradley ("Brad") Pitt was born in Oklahoma. He was the oldest of three children. He went to Kickapoo High School, where he was a good student. After high school, he went to the University of Missouri to study journalism.

But Brad didn't really want to be a journalist; he wanted to act in movies. So, two weeks before college graduation, he got in his car and drove to Hollywood.

Success did not come immediately. For several years, Brad did odd jobs to make money. In one job, for a fast-food restaurant, he dressed up as a giant chicken! Like many other young actors, he also worked as a chauffeur, driving limousines around Los Angeles. In his free time, he took acting classes.

Finally, at age 25, Brad got the role he needed: He was "JD" in the movie *Thelma and Louise.* This helped him start his new career. Other movies, such as *Legends of the Fall* and *Twelve Monkeys,* soon followed. Now he's one of the hottest young stars in Hollywood. He's famous for his good looks. He can get 8 million dollars for one movie.

In real life, Pitt is a private person. He gives very few interviews. "I don't know anything about my favorite actors," he once told an interviewer. "And I don't want people to know about me."

B. Find a word or phrase in the text which means:

1. low-paid, part-time work (paragraph 3): _____

2. very large (paragraph 3): _____

3. a person who drives people's cars (paragraph 3): _____

4. large expensive cars (paragraph 3): _____

5. the character an actor plays in a movie (paragraph 4): _____

6. famous movie actors or singers (paragraph 4): _____

Review

1 Fill in the blanks.

Fill in the blanks. Use words from the box. Use some words more than once.

| do | go | have | make | am | watch | need |

1. Do you want to _____go_____ to a movie on Saturday?

2. I'm going home. I have to _____ my homework.

3. My husband and I usually _____ dinner at five o'clock and eat at six o'clock.

4. We're going to _____ swimming.

5. I can't work today. I _____ a fever.

6. She can't come. She has to _____ to dance class.

7. I _____ an appointment with the doctor. I _____ a backache.

8. Do you want to _____ biking this afternoon?

9. I think I'm sick. I _____ dizzy.

10. Let's _____ TV tonight.

2 Unscramble the sentences.

Write sentences. The first word is capitalized.

1. at / at / o'clock / He / ten / is / usually / work

He is usually at work at ten o'clock.

2. a / in / July / takes / She / usually / vacation

_____

3. a / every / have / I / day / to / wear / uniform

_____

4. a / evening / father / headache / My / has / often / in / the

_____

❸ Match beginnings and endings.

Match the expressions on the left with the correct responses on the right.

1. ___e___   Where were you last night?

2. _____   I'm busy now, but I can help you later.

3. _____   I'm really sorry about that.

4. _____   How about eleven o'clock?

5. _____   I like these. How much are they?

6. _____   What's the matter? You look worried.

7. _____   It's my turn to pay.

8. _____   How do you know Laura?

9. _____   You look familiar.

a. That's OK. I'm not mad at you.

b. So do you. Weren't you at Kate's party last night?

c. No, that's not fair. Let's go Dutch.

d. Seven dollars.

e. At home. Why?

f. Thanks a million.

g. Laura and I were in school together.

h. I am. This homework is really hard.

i. That's a little difficult. I'm going to be in class until twelve.

❹ Complete the puzzle.

Write the simple past tense forms of the verbs in the blanks, and find a mystery word!

1. come
2. get
3. go
4. forget
5. hear
6. have
7. take
8. find
9. feel
10. say
11. meet
12. do
13. tell
14. know
15. see

The mystery word is _____.

⑤ Write questions and answers.

A. Read the letter. As you read, look for the answers to these questions.

1. Who is the letter from? _____

2. Where is she? _____

3. Who is the letter to? (Hint: Look at the last paragraph.) _____

Hi there, guys!

    We're having a great time in California. We're staying with my sister Monica, (the one who's a journalist) in her wonderful house in Beverly Hills! So we're living in style. Monica's at work most of the time, so we can just lie around the pool or play tennis. The weather is wonderful, of course!

    We're going to all the new movies because Monica has to write about them. (Terrible, huh?) Everybody in Hollywood talks about movies all the time. And last week we took a tour around Beverly Hills and saw all the homes of the stars. (Wow!) Then on Saturday we went to Universal Studios. And who do you think we saw? Jack Nicholson! Monica knows him, so she introduced us to him, and he was so nice!

    And of course the food is great. Every evening Monica takes us to a new restaurant to try Thai food, Japanese food, Korean food . . . a different kind every night. It's all good.

    Anyway, I have to go now. Tom and I are going to swim before dinner. I never want to go back to Kansas — or back to work! But I guess I have to! See you all at work next week.

Lots of love,
Kim

B. Now make questions for the following answers.

Questions	Answers
1. Who _is the letter from?_	Kim.
2. Where _____	With her sister Monica.
3. Where _____	They went to Universal Studios.
4. Who _____	Jack Nicholson.
5. What _____	She's going to go back to work.

测试部分

....

Achievement Tests

Jay Maurer
Irene E. Schoenberg

Achievement Tests by
Angela Blackwell

Joan Saslow
Series Director

Preface

This booklet contains Achievement Tests for *True Colors: An EFL Course for Real Communication, Level One*. The Achievement Tests follow the sequence of the Student Book. Each test is designed to be taken upon completion of its corresponding unit in the Student Book.

For ease of scoring, each test is made up of a number of questions divisible into 100. Please refer to the following chart. Simply multiply the number of questions answered incorrectly by the indicated number of points and subtract from 100.

If the test contains	each question is worth
25 questions	4 points
33 questions	3 points

Circle the correct letter.

Example: **A:** What's your name?

       B: _____

         a. Nice to meet you.

         (**b.**) Maria.

1. **A:** Hi. Are you in this class?

     B: _____

       a. I'm Amy Smith.

       b. Yes, I am.

2. **A:** _____

     B: Nice to meet you.

       a. Hi. My name's Bruce.

       b. Nice party.

3. **A:** Nice party.

     B: _____

       a. Yeah, it's great.

       b. Yes, I am.

4. **A:** Sally, this is my friend Steve.

     B: _____

       a. Nice to meet you.

       b. I'm a teacher.

5. **A:** _____

     B: I'm a nurse.

       a. What's your name?

       b. What do you do?

Complete the new sentences. Change the underlined nouns to pronouns. Contract the verbs.

Example: <u>Peter is</u> a doctor.   _____He's_____ a doctor.

6.   <u>Maria is</u> a student.   _____ a student.

7.   <u>Jerome and Annie are</u> my neighbors.   _____ my neighbors.

8.   <u>My parents are</u> teachers.   _____ teachers.

9.   <u>Jan and I are</u> in this class.   _____ in this class.

10.   <u>Bob is</u> an engineer.   _____ an engineer.

Fill in the blanks with words from the box. Use each word only once.

Are	is	he	He's	I	I'm
~~I'm~~	you	your	Who	this	

A: Hi. ___I'm___ Julie, and _____ is my friend Sue. What's _____ name?
                                 11.   **12.**

B: Evan.

A: Nice to meet _____, Evan. _____ you in this class?
                        13.   **14.**

B: Yes, _____ am. _____'s the teacher?
             15.   **16.**

A: Mr. Miller.

B: Is _____ nice?
         17.

A: He's OK. _____ pretty young. Where are you from, Evan?
                   18.

B: _____ from New York.
       19.

A: Hey, Mr. Miller _____ from New York, too!
                          20.

Write the correct occupation below each picture.

a doctor	a lawyer	a nurse	a secretary
an artist	an engineer	a homemaker	~~a student~~

Example:

___a student___

21. _____

22. _____

23. _____

24. _____

25. _____

26. _____

27. _____

Fill in the blanks. Use _a_, _an_, _the_, or no article.

Example: John is ___a___ student. His parents are _____ doctors.

• Eric and Diana are _____ artists. They're from Cleveland. It's _____ city
  28.   **29.**

  in _____ United States.
  30.

• _____ teacher in my class is Tom Brooks. He's _____ good teacher.
  31.   **32.**

• Mike, this is Susan. She's _____ engineer from California.
  33.

Circle the correct letter.

Example: **A:** What's your name?

B: _____

    a. Nice to meet you.

    (b.) Maria.

1. **A:** _____

   B: It's two-fifteen.

    a. What time is it?

    b. Where is it?

2. **A:** Hi, Linda. This is Gary.

   B: _____

    a. What's your name?

    b. Oh, hi! How are you?

3. **A:** How are you?

   B: _____

    a. Nice to meet you.

    b. I'm fine, thanks.

4. **A:** I'm so excited.

   B: _____

    a. How are you?

    b. Excited? Why?

5. **A:** See you later.

   B: _____

    a. Bye.

    b. What time is it?

Fill in the blanks with words from the box. Use each word only once.

are	at	Bye	~~This~~	When
great	See	Why	want	

A: Hello?

B: Hi, Lydia. _____This_____ is Susan.

A: Oh, hi, Susan. How _____ you?
6.

B: Fine. I'm so excited.

A: _____ are you excited?
7.

B: There's a jazz concert _____ the Plaza Theater.
8.

A: That's _____!
9.

B: Do you _____ to go?
10.

A: Maybe. _____ is it?
11.

B: Tonight!

A: OK. _____ you at six o'clock?
12.

B: Terrific. _____.
13.

Write sentences. Use <u>There's</u> or <u>There are</u>.

Example: (snow in Alaska)   *There's snow in Alaska.*

14.   (a good movie at the Lido)   _____

15.   (water in the glass)   _____

16.   (twenty students in my class)   _____

17.   (a soccer game at the stadium)   _____

18.   (three flights every day)   _____

19.   (rice in the bowl)   _____

20.   (burglars in the house)   _____

READING

Read the note. Then circle the correct letter.

Example: The note is from _____.

    a. John

    (b.) Alex and Bill

21.   Alex and Bill are _____.

    a. at a movie

    b. at a party

22.   The movie is _____.

    a. at 7:30

    b. at 9:00

23.   There's a party _____.

    a. at 7:30

    b. at 9:00

24.   The party is _____.

    a. at 24 Bank Street

    b. at John's house

25.   Alex, Bill, and John are _____.

    a. artists

    b. students

John:

7 P.M.

We're at the Lido. There's a good French movie at 7:30. Then there's a party at Kira's house, at about 9:00. She's at 24 Bank Street. See you at the movie, or at the party tonight, or in class tomorrow!

Alex and Bill

Name:

Circle the correct letter.

Example: **A:** What's your name?

B: _____

   a. Nice to meet you.

   (b.) Maria.

1. **A:** _____

   B: Good idea. What's at the Lido?

   a. There's a good movie at the Lido.

   b. Let's go to the movies.

2. **A:** Let's not go out. It's cold.

   B: _____

   a. Oh, all right.

   b. Don't be late.

3. **A:** How about Marco's Pizza?

   B: _____

   a. No, don't call Marco's. Their pizza is terrible!

   b. All right. Let's watch a video instead.

4. **A:** Let's call the movie theater.

   B: _____

   a. OK. How about the movie theater?

   b. Good idea. What's their number?

5. **A:** _____

   B: Sure. S-M-I-T-H.

   a. Your address, please?

   b. Could you spell your name?

Write the correct word in the blank.

Example: Is Bill in ___his___ room?
            <u>his / its</u>

6. _____ name is Andrea. I'm from Chicago.
    <u>Your / My</u>

7. Could you spell _____ name, please?
    <u>your / our</u>

8. Let's go to a restaurant tonight, honey. It's _____ wedding anniversary.
    <u>our / their</u>

9. That's a present for my son. It's _____ birthday tomorrow.
    <u>his / her</u>

10. Hi! I'm John, and this is _____ wife, Norma.
    <u>your / my</u>

11. Jennifer is married. Eric is _____ husband.
    <u>his / her</u>

12. Call Peter. _____ number is 721-8980.
    <u>Your / His</u>

13. The children are at the movies with _____ friends.
    <u>their / her</u>

Write the correct choice below each picture.

| a TV | a computer | a remote |
| a CD player | a cassette player | a VCR |

Example:

___a TV___

14. _____

15. _____

16. _____

17. _____

18. _____

2

Look at the picture. Complete the sentences.

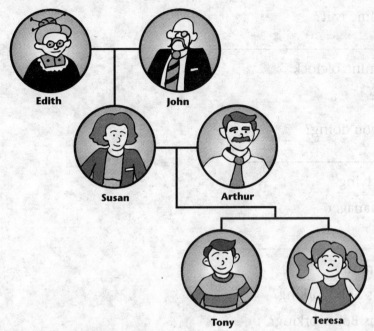

Example: ___Edith___ is Tony's grandmother.

19. _____ is Susan's husband.

20. _____ is Teresa's mother.

21. _____ is Tony's sister.

22. _____ is Teresa's father.

23. _____ is Tony's grandfather.

24. _____ is Arthur's wife.

25. _____ is John and Edith's grandson.

Fill in the blanks with words from the box. Use each word only once.

Sit	Open	go	Go	watch
spell	Call	be	press	

Example: ___Open___ the door, please. It's hot.

26. To leave a message, _____ FIVE now.

27. Let's _____ for a walk.

28. _____ down, please.

29. _____ to the board and write the answer, please.

30. Dinner's at seven. Don't _____ late.

31. _____ me tonight. My number is 450-9216.

32. Could you _____ your name, please?

33. Let's _____ a video tonight.

Circle the correct letter.

Example: **A:** What time is it?

    B: _____

       (**a.**) It's nine o'clock.

       b. Fine.

1.   **A:** What are you doing?

    B: _____

       a. I'm studying.

       b. I'm a manager.

2.   **A:** _____

    B: At a restaurant.

       a. When is Bob working?

       b. Where is Bob working?

3.   **A:** _____

    B: No problem. Go to the corner and turn right.

       a. I'm sorry. I'm lost. I'm going to the post office.

       b. Where are you calling from?

4.   **A:** Where are you calling from?

    B: _____

       a. To the restaurant.

       b. The corner of Seventh Street and Pine Street.

5.   **A:** _____

    B: Yes, I am.

       a. What are you doing?

       b. Are you doing your homework?

6.   **A:** Can I call you back?

    B: _____

       a. I'm sorry.

       b. Sure. No problem.

Look at the pictures. Write sentences. Use subject pronouns. Use activities from the box.

| fixing the car | playing ball | doing his homework | making dinner |
| ~~working~~ | watching TV | talking to a friend | |

Example:  Bob is at Luigi's.

He's working.

7.  Maggie is in the kitchen.

_____

8.  Amy and her grandmother are in the living room.

_____

9.  David is in the garage.

_____

10.  Diana is on the phone.

_____

11.  Sue and Jim are outside.

_____

12.  Steve is in his room.

_____

Fill in the blanks with words from the box. Use each word only once.

| and | between | at | to | Turn | ~~are~~ |

A: Alice? I'm sorry we're late. We're lost. Can you give us directions?

B: Sure. Where _____*are*_____ you calling from?

A: We're at a gas station _____ the corner of Main Street _____ Tenth Avenue.
                                            13.   **14.**

B: OK. Go down Main Street _____ Seventh Avenue. _____ left.
                                            15.   **16.**

   We're on Seventh Avenue _____ Main Street and Church Street.
                                            17.

Rewrite the sentences. Change the underlined words to object pronouns.

Example: I'm having dinner with <u>Jane</u>.   _____*I'm having dinner with her.*_____

18. I'm watching TV with <u>my brothers</u>.   _____

19. Dad's making pizza for <u>my friends and me</u>.   _____

20. Tom's playing ball with <u>John</u>.   _____

21. I'm fixing <u>the car</u>.   _____

22. Mom is calling <u>Amy</u>.   _____

Write questions. Use the present continuous.

Example: What / you / do?   _____*What are you doing?*_____

23. Where / she / go?   _____

24. What / the boys / do?   _____

25. Mary / cook dinner / today?   _____

Circle the correct letter.

Example: **A:** What time is it?

B: _____

- Ⓐ It's nine o'clock.
- **b.** Fine.

1. **A:** _____

B: No, I don't.
- **a.** Do you work?
- **b.** Are you working today?

2. **A:** Do you like your job?

B: _____
- **a.** I work full-time.
- **b.** No, not really.

3. **A:** My brother studies medicine.

B: _____
- **a.** Really? I bet that's tough.
- **b.** Mm-hmm. I work part-time.

4. **A:** Do you study full-time?

B: _____
- **a.** No. I'm only taking two classes.
- **b.** No. I study computers.

5. **A:** What do you study?

B: _____
- **a.** Business.
- **b.** Full-time.

6. **A:** _____

B: Really? I bet that's tough.
- **a.** I'm taking five classes.
- **b.** I'm only taking one class.

Write the correct word in the blank.

Example: I __live__ in San Francisco.
         live / lives

7. My brother _____ a new job.
        have / has

8. _____ your parents have a car?
       Do / Does

9. I _____ sports.
       hate / hates

10. Sarah _____ like rock music.
        don't / doesn't

11. John and Lisa _____ part-time.
        work / works

12. Where _____ Marina live?
        do / does

13. Brett doesn't _____ to school.
        go / goes

14. The children _____ to eat.
        want / wants

15. Does your mother _____ ice cream?
        like / likes

16. _____ they work in an office?
        Do / Does

Write the correct field of study below each picture.

| art | business | dance | ~~computers~~ |
| journalism | math | music | medicine |

Example:

computers

17. _____

18. _____

19. _____

20. _____

21. _____

22. _____

23. _____

Fill in the blanks. Use the simple present tense.

Example: She _____works_____ part-time.
                     work

24. He _____ my class.
            teach

25. Allen _____ pizza.
              love

26. She _____ about me.
              worry

27. Jane _____ a dog.
              have

28. He _____ a lot.
            talk

Complete the questions. Use the simple present tense.

Example: **A:** Who _____lives here_____?

B: John lives here.

A: What _____does Patricia study_____?

B: Patricia studies music.

29. **A:** Where _____?

B: Sam lives in New York.

30. **A:** What time _____?

B: Peter eats breakfast at eight o'clock.

31. **A:** When _____?

B: They work on Mondays.

32. **A:** Where _____?

B: His father works in a restaurant.

33. **A:** Where _____?

B: Ellen works in San Diego.

34. **A:** When _____?

B: Luke exercises at seven o'clock every Friday morning.

READING

Read about Sam. Then mark the statements __true__, __false__, or __I don't know__.

The Ivy Leaves

Sam is a full-time student, but he works part-time in a shoe store. He likes eating out (at Thai and Japanese restaurants) and going to movies. He hates fast food! On Saturday nights, he plays in a jazz band.

Sam is studying business, computers, and Japanese this semester. Why Japanese? "My grandmother lives in Japan, but she often visits us. I want to speak to her in Japanese," he says.

Sam lives at home with his parents, two brothers, and his dog, Rex. Does he have a girlfriend? He doesn't say!

	True	False	I don't know
Example: Sam studies part-time.	☐	☑	☐
35. He likes his job.	☐	☐	☐
36. He likes Thai food.	☐	☐	☐
37. Sam studies on Saturday nights.	☐	☐	☐
38. Sam is taking a Japanese class.	☐	☐	☐
39. Sam lives with his grandmother.	☐	☐	☐
40. Sam has a girlfriend.	☐	☐	☐

Review (Units 1–5): Achievement Test

Name:

Circle the correct letter.

Example: **A:** What time is it?

B: _____

     (**a.**) It's nine o'clock.

     b. Fine.

1. **A:** What's your name?

B: _____

  a. I'm a teacher.

  b. Alex.

2. **A:** Let's watch TV.

B: _____

  a. No, let's rent a video instead.

  b. How about a new TV?

3. **A:** How are you?

B: _____

  a. I'm a student.

  b. Fine, thanks.

4. **A:** Do you like your journalism class?

B: _____

  a. I bet that's fun.

  b. It's hard, but it's interesting.

5. **A:** There's a concert tomorrow. Do you want to go?

B: _____

  a. See you later.

  b. OK.

6. **A:** Rita, this is my friend Paul.

B: _____

  a. Nice to meet you.

  b. Yes, it's great.

7. **A:** Do you want to order a pizza?

B: _____

  a. Good idea. What's the phone number?

  b. OK. Let's go out.

8. **A:** Your address, please?

B: _____

  a. 60 State Street.

  b. Jack Roberts.

9. **A:** Where are you?

B: _____

  a. He's calling from a car.

  b. At the corner of Ninth Avenue and Green Street.

10. **A:** _____

B: I'm a secretary.

  a. Do you work part-time?

  b. What do you do?

Match the questions and the answers. Write the letter in the blank.

Example: ___b___   Do you study full-time?

_____ **11.** Are you studying computers?

_____ **12.** Does Ann work full-time?

_____ **13.** Are they students?

_____ **14.** Do they work full-time?

_____ **15.** Does he like his job?

a. No, they aren't.

b. ~~Yes, I do.~~

c. No, she doesn't.

d. Yes, he does.

e. No, I'm not. I'm studying music.

f. Yes, they do.

Complete the sentences. Use subject or object pronouns.

Example: My father is a lawyer. ___He___ works in an office.

16. My mother is a teacher. _____ teaches art.

17. My brother lives in Chicago. I talk to _____ on the phone every week.

18. Julie and her husband like pizza. _____ order in every Friday.

19. Andrea and Amy are going to the concert. I want to go with _____.

20. Amy and I like sports. _____ play soccer together.

21. I'm going to see "War of the Worlds" at the Lido. Do you want to come with _____?

22. My VCR is broken. Can you fix _____?

Write the correct word in the blank.

Example: Could you spell ___your___ name, please?
                           my / your

23. Peter is married. _____ wife's name is Millie.
                        Her / His

24. Call me. _____ phone number is 867-2234.
                My / Your

25. My mother and father live in New York. _____ apartment is on Eighth Avenue.
                                            My / Their

26. My sister is a doctor. _____ office is at Fifth Street and Green Street.
                             His / Her

Complete the sentences with activities from the box. Use the present continuous and contractions.

~~talk to a friend~~   cook dinner   play soccer   work

Example: Jason is on the phone. He's *talking to a friend*. _____

27.   Bob's in the kitchen. He _____.

28.   Sally's at her office. She _____.

29.   Jane and Tina are in the living room. They _____.

30.   Sam and Eric are outside. They _____.

Fill in the blanks. Use the simple present tense.

Example: She ____works____ full-time.
                     work

31.   My brother _____ in New York.
                         live

32.   My friends _____ basketball on
                           play
Fridays.

33.   My sister _____ a new CD player.
                          have

34.   Where's John? I _____ him.
                             not / see

Complete the questions. Use the simple present tense.

Example: **A:** What ____does Peter play____?
              B: Peter plays soccer.

35.   **A:** Where _____?
          B: His father works in an office.

36.   **A:** What time _____?
          B: Ellen eats breakfast at seven o'clock.

37.   **A:** Where _____?
          B: I live in Los Angeles.

38.   **A:** When _____?
          B: She excercises every morning.

Fill in the blanks. Use a, an, the, or no article.

Jane is _____a_____ student. She studies _____ computers at Central University. She lives

(39.)

in _____ apartment. _____ apartment is very small. There is _____ living room,

(40.)   (41.)   (42.)

but no dining room. There is _____ table in the living room. There are always _____

(43.)   (44.)

books on _____ table. Jane likes to do her homework there. She is very studious. Jane

(45.)

doesn't have _____ TV. She says she doesn't have time to watch TV.

(46.)

READING

Read about Sara. Then mark the statements true, false, or I don't know.

Sara is a secretary. She works full-time, and she studies part-time. She works in a lawyer's office. She is studying math. She wants to be an engineer. Sara is very busy. She studies every day. She goes to class two nights a week. Sara lives alone. Her family lives in a different city, but her sister visits her often. Sara doesn't have a boyfriend right now, but she has many friends.

		True	False	I don't know
Example:	Sara is a lawyer.	☐	☑	☐
47.	Sara works full-time.	☐	☐	☐
48.	Sara goes to school on Wednesday.	☐	☐	☐
49.	Sara has a brother.	☐	☐	☐
50.	Sara has a boyfriend.	☐	☐	☐

Circle the correct letter.

A: What time is it?

B: _____

    (**a.**) It's nine o'clock.

    b. Fine.

1. **A:** Doctor's office.

B: _____

    a. I'm Sam Johnson.

    b. Hello. This is Sam Johnson.

2. **A:** How can I help you?

B: _____

    a. I need an appointment.

    b. Fine, thank you.

3. **A:** Thank you.

B: _____

    a. You're welcome.

    b. That's fine.

4. **A:** _____

B: Yes, that's fine. Thank you.

    a. Can I help you?

    b. How about 3:15 tomorrow?

5. **A:** _____

B: Yes, 4:30 is fine.

    a. I need an appointment.

    b. Is 4:30 a possibility?

Label the parts of the body. Use the words in the box.

back	shoulder	arm	knee
~~ankle~~	hand	wrist	

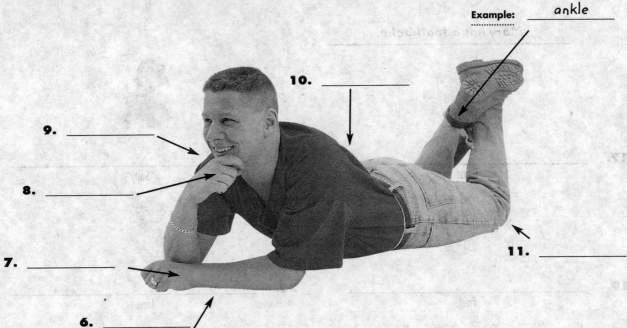

Example: _____ankle_____

9. _____

10. _____

8. _____

7. _____

6. _____

11. _____

Complete the sentences about the future. Use <u>be going to</u>.

Example: This evening, I _m going to do my homework_____.
                                    do my homework

12. We_____ this Saturday.
                    clean the house

13. Tonight, Sandy_____.
                              rent a video

14. This evening, they_____.
                                  not / go out to eat

15. We_____ next month.
                    take a vacation

16. It_____ today.
              not / rain

Look at the pictures. Write sentences about the people.

Example:

Mary has a toothache.

17. _____
David

18. _____
Sally

19. _____
Paul

20. _____
Jane

21. _____
Andy

Rewrite the sentences. Use the frequency adverb in parentheses.

Example: I do my homework. (always)   _____I always do my homework._____

22. We go to restaurants. (never)   _____

23. Steven is late for work. (always)   _____

24. My parents get up early. (often)   _____

25. The teachers give homework. (rarely)   _____

Name:

Circle the correct letter.

Example: **A:** What time is it?

B: _____

     (a.) It's nine o'clock.

     b. Fine.

1. **A:** Let's go hiking this weekend.

B: _____

     a. Sorry, I have to hike.

     b. Sorry, I have to study for a test.

2. **A:** I'm sorry. I can't go to the movie with you.

B: _____

     a. OK. Maybe some other time.

     b. Why don't you ask Sheila?

3. **A:** _____

B: I can't understand my chemistry homework.

     a. Can you help me?

     b. What's the matter?

4. **A:** I'm sorry. I can't help you now.

B: _____

     a. What's the matter?

     b. What about later? Please?

5. **A:** _____

B: Good idea.

     a. I can't go fishing tomorrow.

     b. Let's go fishing on Saturday.

6. **A:** OK, I can help you later.

B: _____

     a. Thanks a million.

     b. What about later?

Look at the pictures. Write the correct phrase from the box in the first blank and the correct verb form in the second blank.

~~go fishing~~	go hiking	go biking
go rollerblading	go swimming	

Example:

A: Let's _____*go fishing*_____ today.

B: I can't. I _____*have to*_____ work.
　　　　　　 have / have to

A: Let's _____ today.
　　　　　　 7.

B: I can't. I _____ a chemistry test today.
　　　　8. have / have to

A: Let's _____.
　　　　　　 9.

B: I can't. I _____ study for a history test.
　　　　10. have / have to

A: Let's _____.
　　　　　　 11.

B: I can't. I _____ go to English class.
　　　　12. have / have to

A: Let's _____ this afternoon.
　　　　　　 13.

B: I can't. I _____ math class at 2:00.
　　　　14. have / have to

Look at Mary's calendar. Write **T** (true) or **F** (false) next to the statements.

Tuesday 12

8:00: drive Tony to school
9–12: work
6:00: dinner at Mario's restaurant

Wednesday 13

9–5: work
6:30: dance class

Thursday 14

10:00: doctor
12–5: work

Example: _____F_____   Mary has to work on Tuesday afternoon.

_____ **15.** Mary has to get up before 8:00 on Tuesday morning.

_____ **16.** Mary has to make dinner on Tuesday.

_____ **17.** Mary can go to the movies at 6:00 on Wednesday night.

_____ **18.** Mary has to go to the doctor at 10:00 on Thursday morning.

_____ **19.** Mary can't pick up her son from school on Thursday at 4:00.

_____ **20.** Mary has to work on Thursday afternoon.

Look at the pictures. Write sentences about these people. Use <u>can</u> or <u>can't</u>.

Example:

Bonjour!

Anna can speak French.

21. Anna/speak French

Buon giorno!

22. Rex/speak Italian

23. Bruno/touch his toes

Maria/ski

24.

Kate and Kelly/swim

25.

John and Helen/dance the samba

Unit Eight: Achievement Test

Name:

Circle the correct letter.

Example: **A:** _____

B: Fine.

   a. What are you doing?

   (b.) How are you?

1. **A:** _____

B: Yes? How can I help you?

   a. Do you have any umbrellas?

   b. Excuse me.

2. **A:** Do you have any sweaters?

B: _____

   a. How much are they?

   b. Yes. Right this way.

3. **A:** _____

B: $12.99

   a. How much is it?

   b. How can I help you?

4. **A:** The jacket is only $57.00.

B: _____

   a. OK. I'll take it.

   b. Sure.

5. **A:** How can I help you?

B: _____

   a. Right this way.

   b. Do you have any boots?

1

Fill in the blanks with words from the box. Use each word only once.

| some | that | ~~one~~ | it | it | they | those |

A: Can I help you?

B: Yes. I'm looking for a dress shirt.

A: How about this ___one___? It's on sale—only $25.00.

B: Hmm . . . I think I prefer _____ one over there. How much is _____?
6. 7.

A: It's $29.99.

B: I'll take _____. Now, I'm also looking for _____ shoes.
8. 9.

A: What size do you wear?

B: Size 10. Do you have these in black?

A: We don't have them in black. But _____ brown shoes in the corner are very nice.
10.

They're on sale today.

B: OK. Let me see them. How much are _____?
11.

A: $46.95.

Look at the picture. Write **T** (true) *or* **F** (false) *next to the statements.*

Allen   **Jane**

Example: _____F_____ Jane is wearing a nightgown.

_____ **12.** Allen is wearing a suit.

_____ **13.** Allen is wearing a dress shirt.

_____ **14.** Allen is wearing a belt.

_____ **15.** Allen and Jane are wearing running shoes.

_____ **16.** Jane is wearing a skirt and a blouse.

_____ **17.** Jane is wearing a windbreaker.

_____ **18.** Jane is wearing socks and sandals.

Fill in the blanks. Use __some__ or __any__.

Example: I have _____some_____ friends.

There isn't _____any_____ time.

19. Ray has _____ CDs.

20. Ray doesn't have _____ CDs.

21. There isn't _____ food in the house.

22. I need _____ help.

23. I don't need _____ help.

24. We don't have _____ money.

25. There are _____ calls for you.

Circle the correct letter.

Example: **A:** _____

B: Fine.

    a. What are you doing?

    (b.) How are you?

1. **A:** Oops! I'm sorry.

  B: _____

    a. That's OK!

    b. Excuse me.

2. **A:** By the way, I'm Karen.

  B: _____

    a. That's OK!

    b. Hi, Karen. I'm John.

3. **A:** _____

  B: Yes, I was. Were you?

    a. Weren't you at Maria's party last week?

    b. You look familiar.

4. **A:** _____

  B: We were friends in high school.

    a. Was Maria there?

    b. How do you know Maria?

5. **A:** That's OK. Don't worry about it.

  B: _____

    a. No, really, I'm sorry about that.

    b. Excuse me.

Fill in the blanks. Use <u>was</u>, <u>wasn't</u>, <u>were</u>, or <u>weren't</u>.

Yesterday _____*was*_____ our wedding anniversary, but the evening _____ pretty bad.
                                                                                      6.

First, we _____ late for the movie. And the movie _____ very good—in fact it
              7.   **8.**

_____ terrible. Then all the restaurants _____ closed because it _____
  9.   **10.**   **11.**

Sunday. We _____ every happy!
                12.

Rewrite the sentences. Use the past tense.

Example: I'm at Mary Ann's house.   ____*I was at Mary Ann's house.*____

13.   Where are you?   _____

14.   Is there a test?   _____

15.   There aren't many people here.   _____

16.   Isn't it a beautiful day?   _____

17.   Why aren't you in school?   _____

18.   There's a movie at seven o'clock.   _____

Fill in the blanks with words from the box. Use each word only once.

assistant	boss	boyfriend	fiancés
neighbors	partner	~~husband~~	roommates

Example: Betty and David are married. David is Betty's _____ *husband* _____.

19. Ron and Adela are going to get married. They are _____.

20. Jim and Daphne are dating. Jim is Daphne's _____.

21. The Butlers live near us. They are our _____.

22. My boss has a lot of work. She needs a(n) _____.

23. Joan and Sara live in an apartment together. They are _____.

24. My father and Mr. Chen have a restaurant together. Mr. Chen is my
father's _____.

25. I like my job, but sometimes my _____ gives me too much work.

Write the correct word in the blank.

Example: I'm going to visit ____*my*____ cousins.

              my / mine

• This isn't _____ class. _____ is on the third floor.

        26. your / yours   **27.** Your / Yours

• I'm giving these videos to Jane. They're _____ .

                              28. her / hers

• The cars are the same, except _____ car is red and _____ is green.

                     29. our / ours   **30.** their / theirs

• My uncle always parks _____ car in front of _____ house.

                   31. his / her   **32.** our / ours

• Put _____ gloves on. It's cold outside.

     33. your / yours

Circle the correct letter.

Example: **A:** _____

         B: Fine.

            a. What are you doing?

            (b.) How are you?

1.   **A:** Mandy. Hi. It's Jim.

      B: _____

         a. Jim! Guess who?

         b. Jim! When did you get back?

2.   **A:** When did you get back?

      B: _____

         a. Mexico.

         b. Last week.

3.   **A:** _____

      B: Great! We had a very good time.

         a. So how was the vacation?

         b. So where was the vacation?

4.   **A:** _____

      B: We saw a lot of movies and went to the theater.

         a. What did you do?

         b. How was the movie?

5.   **A:** We lay on the beach, went swimming, and ate good food.

      B: _____

         a. How was the vacation?

         b. Sounds like you had a good time.

Rewrite the sentences. Use the past tense.

Example: I feel sick.   I felt sick.

6.   They come home at four o'clock.   _____

7.   We have a house at the beach.   _____

8.   My father says hello.   _____

9.   My mother makes my clothes.   _____

10.   The children don't eat vegetables.   _____

11.   She meets him every evening.   _____

12.   He doesn't get home early.   _____

13.   I don't see it.   _____

14.   We go to school at nine o'clock.   _____

15.   She tells the truth.   _____

Complete the questions in the simple past tense. Use the indicated words.

Example: When _____ did you arrive _____ ?
                               you / arrive

16.   How _____ the answer?
                 you / know

17.   Where _____ yesterday?
                 Pattie / go

18.   What _____ last night?
                 you / do

19.   Why _____ me?
                 you / call

20.   When _____ that movie?
                 Alex / see

READING

Read the essay. Then mark the statements <u>true</u>, <u>false</u>, or <u>I don't know</u>.

My Grandfather
by Christa Barkley

    My grandfather's name was Jan Cywinski. He was born in Poland in 1902, but his family moved to the United States when he was twelve. They lived in Chicago in an area where everyone spoke Polish. His parents never spoke English well. But my grandfather studied hard and eventually graduated with honors from the University of Chicago. He met my grandmother, Anna, when he was a student, and they married in 1924. They had six children, one of whom was my mother.

		True	False	I don't know
Example:	Jan is alive now.	☐	☑	☐
21.	Jan was born in Chicago.	☐	☐	☐
22.	Jan's parents couldn't speak English well.	☐	☐	☐
23.	Jan was a good student.	☐	☐	☐
24.	Anna was also a student.	☐	☐	☐
25.	Jan was the father of Christa's mother.	☐	☐	☐

Circle the correct letter.

Example: **A:** What time is it?

B: _____

(**a.**) It's nine o'clock.

b. Fine.

1. **A:** _____

   B: You're welcome.

   a. How are you?

   b. Thank you.

2. **A:** _____

   B: Don't worry about it.

   a. I'm sorry about that.

   b. Can you help me?

3. **A:** _____

   B: Sorry, I have to finish my homework.

   a. I can't go to the movies with you.

   b. Let's go to the movies.

4. **A:** We spent several great days at the beach.

   B: _____

   a. Sounds like you had a good time.

   b. So how was the vacation?

5. **A:** Can you drive me to school tomorrow?

   B: _____

   a. I can't. I have to go to work early.

   b. I can't right this minute.

6. **A:** Can I help you?

   B: _____

   a. Excuse me.

   b. Do you have any T-shirts?

7. **A:** How much is it?

   B: _____

       a. OK. I'll take it.

       b. It's $16.98.

8. **A:** When did you get back?

   B: _____

       a. We had a great time.

       b. Monday.

9. **A:** I need an appointment right away.

   B: _____

       a. Is tomorrow morning OK?

       b. I have a headache.

10. **A:** Let's go swimming.

   B: _____

       a. Sorry. I can't swim.

       b. Great idea. Let's go to the theater.

Write sentences. Use the present tense and the frequency adverb in parentheses.

Example: I / exercise / in the morning (usually)   _I usually exercise in the morning._

11. We / order / a pizza (occasionally)   _____

12. Sandra / answer / questions in class (often) _____

13. Jack / be / on time for work (always)   _____

14. I / worry / about tests (sometimes)   _____

Complete the sentences about the future. Use <u>be</u> <u>going</u> <u>to</u> and contractions if possible.

Example: We _'re going to take a vacation_ next month.
                   take a vacation

15. Tomorrow I _____ in the gym.
                  play volleyball

16. Tonight my mother and father _____.
                       go out to a restaurant

17. Tomorrow morning I _____ early.
                  not / get up

18. Tonight Robert _____.
               make dinner

Look at Tina's calendar.

Monday 10	Tuesday 11	Wednesday 12
9–5: work 6:00: go to school	9–12: work 3:00: go to the doctor 6:00: make supper	9–5: work 6:00: go to the bank 8:00: do homework

What does Tina have to do? Write sentences about Tina.

Example: Monday at 6:00 in the evening   *She has to go to school.*

19. Tuesday at 3:00 in the afternoon

20. Tuesday at 6:00 in the evening

21. Wednesday at 6:00 in the evening

22. Wednesday at 8:00 in the evening

Complete the sentences. Use verbs in the simple past tense.

Example: He didn't move to California. He ____moved____ to Florida.

23. I didn't meet my boyfriend at school. I _____ him at work.

24. I didn't play the piano yesterday. But I _____ the piano every day last week.

25. He didn't go to school in New York. He _____ to school in Chicago.

26. He didn't call his mother. He _____ his aunt.

27. I didn't have a sore neck. I _____ a sore back.

Complete the questions. Use the simple past tense.

Example: When _____*did Peter leave*_____ ?
                 Peter left at eleven o'clock.

28. **A:** What _____ ?

    B: They saw "Star Wars."

29. **A:** When _____ ?

    B: Lily did her homework last night.

30. **A:** What sport _____ ?

    B: Pelé played soccer.

31. **A:** Where _____ ?

    B: We went to Acapulco.

FILL in the blanks. Use <u>some</u> or <u>any</u>.

32. I don't have _____ running shoes.

33. I want to buy _____ presents for my brothers and sisters.

34. There are _____ shirts on sale.

35. There aren't _____ shoes on sale.

READING

Read about Kate and Steve. Then mark the statements <u>true</u>, <u>false</u>, or <u>I don't know</u>.

Kate and Steve were married last Saturday. They didn't meet at work. They didn't meet at school. They didn't meet through friends. They met through a video dating service.

Kate and Steve each made a video. They talked about their favorite things. A woman at the dating service made a video tape of each of them. Kate talked about dancing and hiking. Steve talked about music and swimming. They both talked about their love of skiing.

At the dating service, Kate and Steve looked at many videos. But Kate liked Steve the best. And Steve liked Kate the best. They had their first date about a year ago. They were fiancés for six months. Now they plan to have a happy life together.

		True	False	I don't know
Example:	Steve and Kate met at work.	☐	☑	☐
36.	Both Steve and Kate went to a video dating service.	☐	☐	☐
37.	Both Steve and Kate made videos.	☐	☐	☐
38.	Steve likes rock music.	☐	☐	☐
39.	Kate likes skiing.	☐	☐	☐
40.	Steve and Kate are going to get married.	☐	☐	☐